The
Pasteboard
Bandit

The Pasteboard Bandit

Arna Bontemps
and Langston Hughes

Illustrations by Peggy Turley

Introduction by Alex Bontemps
Afterword by Cheryl A. Wall

Oxford University Press
New York • Oxford

Oxford University Press

Oxford   New York
Athens Auckland Bangkok Bogotá Bombay
Buenos Aires Calcutta Cape Town Dar es Salaam Delhi
Florence Hong Kong Istanbul Karachi
Kuala Lumpur Madras Madrid Melbourne
Mexico City Nairobi Paris Singapore
Taipei Tokyo Toronto Warsaw
and associated companies in
Berlin Ibadan

Published by Oxford University Press, Inc.,
198 Madison Avenue, New York, New York 10016

Oxford is a registered trademark of Oxford University Press

The Pasteboard Bandit is published courtesy of the James Weldon Johnson Memorial
Collection, Beinecke Rare Book and Manuscript Library, Yale University.

Design: Nora Wertz

Library of Congress Cataloging-in-Publication Data
Bontemps, Arna Wendell, 1902–1973.
The pasteboard bandit / by Arna Bontemps and Langston Hughes; illustrations by Peggy
Turley; introduction by Alex Bontemps; afterword by Cheryl A. Wall.
p. cm. — (The Iona and Peter Opie library of children's literature)
ISBN 0-19-511476-0
[1. Friendship—Fiction. 2. Toys—Fiction. 3. Mexico—Fiction.]
I. Hughes, Langston, 1902–1967. II. Turley, Peggy, ill.
III. Title. IV. Series
PZ7.B6443Pas   1997
[Fic]—dc21   97-11626
CIP

1 3 5 7 9 8 6 4 2

Printed in Hong Kong
on acid-free paper

CONTENTS

INTRODUCTION

ALEX BONTEMPS

My father, Arna Bontemps, once wrote, "The poet who ignores children does so at his peril. And the one who treats them as little monsters may one day be assaulted by them." *The Pasteboard Bandit*, which my father wrote with Langston Hughes in 1935, represents the period when he began to discover his voice as a writer of stories for children. Yet despite the success of their first children's book, *Popo and Fifina*, published three years earlier, they were not able to get *The Pasteboard Bandit* published during their lifetimes. Its publication now, more than 60 years after they wrote it, is cause for celebration.

It was perhaps natural that both Langston and my father had a great interest in books for children and wrote so well for them. When my father was a child, reading was his only outlet from a sense of loss following his mother's death and from what seemed to him an oppressively religious family. He started reading Robert Louis Stevenson at a very early age, and the fact that he went to school in the redwood country of northern California where Stevenson wrote really clicked on his storytelling light. And he always remembered the connection between the love of reading and the love of writing.

Hughes was one of the modern poets who, my father thought, had not abandoned children, either in his affections or in his writing. My own recollections of Hughes confirm that impression. From the moment that I met Langston, I saw that he was one of those adults who have the ability to relate to children. We were in a crowded room, but he seemed to be making contact with me as an equal. Hughes had the child in him, and children really zeroed in on him. It was unmistakable, something in his eye, something I knew even before he talked to me.

Both men were teachers. Hughes taught for a time at the Lab School in Chicago. My father taught high school before he became the librarian at Fisk University. As a matter of fact, he met my mother teaching at Harlem Academy. And both of them did a lot of readings for children—my father probably more than Langston, but not much more.

By the time I was born, my father and Langston had become very close and remained so throughout their lives. Hughes frequently traveled through the South lecturing and so it was convenient for him to visit my father in Nashville. And my father made an effort as often as he could to go to New York, where Langston lived. They had different contacts and different interests, so at a professional level they were very helpful to one another. But also, their temperaments were almost made for one another. My father was a very patient and very genuinely affable person, and so was Langston. There was no ego, never any tension, and I think that's why they bonded and held together for so long.

The success of *Popo and Fifina* in the 1930s marked a turning point in my father's literary development. Both he and Hughes loved children—of course, my dad and mom had six of their own—and my dad was a teacher for most of his life. But for my father, children's literature became a serious and ongoing outlet for his creative energy, as serious as novels or any other form of writing.

By writing for children, my father also thought he was serving some larger social and cultural purpose. He felt that in terms of having an effect on how people felt about each other, children's literature was the best way to go. Certainly, he felt that it could be effective in influencing how people felt about blacks, and about how we felt about each other and our experience in America. But he wanted to reach people beyond just the black community. For my father—and I would think also for Langston—the promise he saw in writing for children was that "they readily identify with all other children (as they do also with animals)." This is why, I believe, he never considered any of his writing for children to be for blacks only, even when they featured black characters in black communities.

This is also why, I think, he felt free to write stories about children who were not black, believing that children by and large had not been contaminated by racism and would be able to identify with other children no matter what their color or ethnicity. *The Pasteboard Bandit*, for example, has no black characters—it is about a Mexican boy and a white boy—but it demonstrates how people need to cross boundaries and borders in order to know each other.

My father took great satisfaction from the letters he received from kids who had read his books. He would invariably share these letters with us at breakfast, something that was out of character for him. He never voluntarily spoke about awards or honors that he had received. But if there was a fan letter from a child, he would always mention it.

My father would be elated to see *The Pasteboard Bandit* finally brought to press. He was convinced that his books for children had life. He would be delighted to have his idea confirmed that children's literature—like any other "good" writing —had a universality and a timelessness that would sustain it long after the author's life had ended.

CHAPTER 1

THE MAN WITH
THE RABBIT WHISKERS

HE WAS ONLY SIX INCHES TALL, and there were many people who hadn't even noticed him at the fair. But that did not matter to Tito. He knew that by and by somebody would come along and pay attention to his big white sombrero, his shaggy hair, his bushy black whiskers and his little round eyes. Somebody, he was sure, would admire the way he clinched his tiny fists and held one hand in the air, making a strong gesture.

Tito was willing to wait. Of course there were many pasteboard men at the fair. Many of them were much larger than he. Some wore

brighter clothes. Some had bigger sombreros. All this Tito knew. Even on the shelf where he stood under the bright awning there were tall figures who tried to push in front of the brave little bandit so that he could not be seen. Yet Tito was not impatient. He felt sure that his time would come.

The sun was bright that day. Many people had come to the plaza. Some were shooting firecrackers. Some were eating candy. Some were throwing rings and guessing numbers at the prize booths. And some were just sitting on the benches. All of them seemed to enjoy the day.

The Indian woman who kept the booth where Tito and the other pasteboard toys stood wore a cherry-colored waist and a skirt like a pumpkin flower. Her hair was braided into two long ropes that hung down her back. Her husband sat on a stool with a bright red serape thrown across his shoulders. His face was the color and shape of a brown pottery jug. They had no children. That is why the woman looked so happy when a small bright-eyed boy came up to the booth and began looking at the figurines.

"How do you like my pasteboard toys?" she asked him.

He shrank away a little, for he was very shy, and answered so softly she could scarcely hear what he said.

"They're fine."

"Would you like to buy one?"

He didn't know how to answer that. He wanted one very much, but he had only a nickel in his pocket and he hated to spend it for a thing that looked like a doll, even though it was actually a bandit and dressed in bright clothes. He intended to buy candy with his big copper coin.

"I don't know," he said.

The Indian woman leaned across the counter and took his hand.

"What is your name?'

"Juanito," he told her. "Juanito Pérez."

"Where do you live?"

The boy turned and pointed to some houses high on the side of the hill. One, a very small one, was painted bright green.

"There," Juanito said. "My papá is the man who paints gourds and pottery to sell at the fiestas."

"Yes, yes, I know. Well, are you a good boy, Juanito?"

Again he bowed his head and shrank away shyly. Of course he was a good boy, but he couldn't say he was. Fortunately, a man who sat nodding on a nearby stool opened his eyes at that moment and answered for him.

"Certainly he's a good boy, Consuelo," he said. "Don't you see how polite he is? Give him a toy if he wants one."

Juanito's heart beat hard. Did the man mean he would give him one *free?* Had he understood the man?

"All right," the woman said. "Which one do you like best, Juanito? Look at all of them and tell me which one you like."

Tito, from his shelf, heard the last words very distinctly. This was his chance, he thought. He looked down at the little brown boy and tried to think how it would feel to belong to such a polite little fellow. Tito couldn't move, but he tried to look as important as he could, tried to clinch his little pasteboard fists even tighter, but it did no good. There was a big fat man beside him, a man who seemed much more impressive in his brick-red suit, his lavender sombrero and his glossy pointed whiskers. On the other side there stood a huge stupid-looking fellow with a long nose and a funny little yellow jacket. Tito was sure he would not be seen between two pasteboard men so much larger than himself.

Yet, he *did* like that little boy named Juanito. It would be fine if—

Ah, the little boy was looking straight at Tito, looking straight into his bright round eyes. And, yes, he was smiling.

"I think," Juanito said, pointing his finger, "I think I like that small one with the blue coat and the bushy rabbit whiskers."

"Oh, the little bandit," the brown woman said. "Well, I think that's a good choice. He seems to be such a brave little man. He is yours, Juanito. Show him to your father when you go home."

"Thank you," Juanito said, taking the pasteboard figure in his hands. "Thank you very, very much."

He started down the road, passing the other booths and the places where games were being played, forgetting about the candy he intended to buy, paying no attention to the merry-go-round on the corner. He was thinking that maybe he and Tito might become good friends.

People with suitcases were getting out of the bus at the next corner, people who had come to Taxco from Cuernavaca and Mexico City, but Juanito did not stop. He had promised the señora in the booth that he would show Tito to his father, and he intended to keep his word.

When he was halfway up the hill, he paused to catch his breath and look down on the dense green plaza. He could still hear the music of the merry-go-round, still hear the voices of people standing in front of the tall church and of others playing games at the fair. But the things down there did not seem to matter so much now that Juanito had Tito. With no brothers or sisters of his own, a friend like Tito could make a lot of difference. Juanito was almost out of breath when he reached the green house on the hill, but he knew he was one of the happiest little Indian boys in Taxco that afternoon.

CHAPTER 2

JUANITO MAKES
A FRIEND

At first Tito felt like a stranger in the small green house on the side of the hill, a house belonging to real people. He had never been in a house before, and here there were no other little pasteboard men to keep him company.

The inside of the house, too, was something of a disappointment at first. The furniture was very simple, just a table in the center of the living room and a few chairs around the wall. Tito could only peep into the other rooms from his place on the table, but he could see that they had in them no more than was absolutely necessary for rooms to have. He began to think that maybe Juanito's family was very poor. But, of course, he knew that that did not matter if they were kind and polite.

There was no clock on the wall, so Tito began to wonder what time it was. There were voices in the kitchen. What was going on? Tito couldn't even tell whether it was night or day. But a few minutes later somebody opened the kitchen door and he found out. Señor Pérez, his wife and his little son, Juanito, were at breakfast.

They did not talk much as they ate, and when they spoke their voices were soft.

"Well, Juanito," the father said, "what will you do with yourself today?"

The boy bowed his head and thought a long while. Then he said, "There is a strange American family in the red house down the road. Maybe I'll walk down there and say hello."

"Strangers, you say?"

The mother put another tortilla on his plate.

"They just came yesterday," she said. "They seem to be artists."

"Artists, artists, artists. Taxco is getting full of them," exclaimed the father.

"Aren't you an artist, papá?" Juanito asked.

"Well, yes. But not the same kind. Artists are fine, I only mean I'm afraid there are too many of us in this little town. Maybe, though, you'd better not bother them if they're busy painting."

For a few more minutes Juanito ate in silence. His mother, who was barefooted, went outdoors and returned with a cup of cool water from the well. When she came back she sat down and began eating the egg on her plate.

"I wouldn't bother the people any if they're busy," Juanito said. "I only thought maybe I'd show them Tito."

The two older people laughed softly. Tito heard it all from the front room. That Juanito, his mother and father thought, he was surely some boy. There he was wanting to show that new American family a little pasteboard bandit that didn't cost more than a nickel. Juanito—what a boy he was—thinking little Tito worth showing to those tourist people who had just come to town.

All this talk made the tiny bandit himself feel very sad. Why, he wondered, was it so funny for Juanito to be proud of his toy? Why did they think people would not appreciate a brave little man like himself?

"Tito is a fine little fellow," the father said. "But he's just a toy."

"Maybe," Juanito suggested timidly, "maybe I could show him to the little boy."

"They have a little boy?"

Juanito and his mother both assured the father that the new family did have a little son, and a bright looking one, too.

"Well, now, maybe that's different," Señor Pérez smiled.

Tito began to feel much happier. It was good to know Juanito appreciated his worth, if nobody else did. Now perhaps the little American boy would see tiny brave Tito; perhaps—if Tito made a very, very good impression—even the mother and father might take him into their house, hold him in their hands and examine his little blue coat, his red girdle, the white buttons down the side of his pant legs, his furious little rabbit beard. What an experience for Tito!

Breakfast was over and the doors and windows were thrown open to let in sunlight and a fresh breeze. Little Tito saw the fig trees in the yard, saw the chickens scratching just outside the door, and he could hardly wait for Juanito to take him visiting. He clinched his tiny fists tighter and tighter. Then he began to think.

Surely this was no way to behave. A little toy bandit could not make time fly faster by clinching his fists and working himself up. No, he should always be patient. "I must learn to control myself," he said. "I must not fly into a temper. My time will come. Juanito has not forgotten me."

And Tito was right. Juanito finished helping his mother in the kitchen and came into the front room for his little friend. Carrying him carefully, he went across the patio, out the front door, and down the narrow little street on the side of the hill.

The morning was fine. The plaza was greener than ever. The fair was still going on, but there were not so many people there today. Once more an automobile bus was unloading in front of the church. The cathedral seemed taller than ever against the clear blue sky. Juanito passed many small poor houses, passed a few large fine ones and came to a red one that was neither small nor large, neither poor nor fine, but something in between. A small American boy was standing in the door.

Looking very solemn, feeling very shy, Juanito bowed his head, scraping his bare toes in the dirt. When he looked up he saw the strange child coming toward him, so Juanito took a few more steps. Tito understood. He began to feel quite happy. When they were facing each other on the path, the little blond stranger pointed to himself and whispered, "Kenny."

18

"Juanito," the little Indian boy answered.

"Come," said Kenny, starting up the path.

"*Vamanos*," Juanito said, following him.

Then both boys paused and Kenny pointed to the little pasteboard bandit. There was a question in his eye.

"Tito," Juanito said.

The little bandit could almost feel himself puffing out with pride.

Kenny's father and mother left their easels and came to the door with their paint boards on their arms, their buff-colored smocks smeared with finger marks. The father could talk Juanito's language. He said good morning in Spanish.

"*Buenos dias*," Juanito answered.

The mother smiled and said something in English that Juanito did not understand. But Tito knew that it was, "What a nice little Mexican boy! He will be a fine playmate for Kenny."

And Tito agreed with that.

CHAPTER 3

TITO TUMBLES

Then for a handful of days Tito stood on a shelf in Juanito's bedroom, half-forgotten. Dust collected on the brave little man's shoulders. A tiny speck of paint peeled off one of his clinched fists. But time passed rapidly, and one day Juanito came into the house from his play, stood in a chair and took Tito down from the shelf.

Kenny was in the patio waiting. The two boys were now able to talk pretty well, using a little of Juanito's language and a little of Kenny's. But since Tito could understand both languages, it made no difference at all to him.

They sat beside the well, with Tito between them on the low stone fence.

"*Abeja!*" said Juanito as a fierce little creature came zooming over the wall of the courtyard.

"A bumble-bee," Kenny said.

But as quickly as he had come, the bee was gone. Tito felt a trifle nervous, standing there on the well-stone, looking down into the water. A bee darting about so fast in the patio, not noticing where he was going, might accidentally zoom right into little pasteboard Tito. It was too horrible to think about. That bee might knock him off the stone fence and into—oh, it would be better not to think about it at all.

"Where is your father?" Kenny asked. "I thought he was going to paint his pottery vases this morning."

"He's in his room," Juanito said. "He's waiting for the man who brings the pottery. See," Juanito pointed to the corner of the courtyard where his father usually worked, "he has nothing else to paint, no bowls or jars or dishes, nothing. Not even a gourd."

"Will the man come soon?"

"Maybe today, maybe *mañana*," Juanito said. "*Quién sabe?* I don't know."

Just at that moment something bumped against the swinging doors of the patio. Then, as they flew open, a little calf ran in from the street. He had no business there, as he did not belong to Juanito's father.

The boys left Tito on the well-stone and began chasing the frisky young animal round and round the courtyard. As they ran the calf bounded about, kicked up his heels and circled the well dangerously near Tito, passing the gate and making circles again.

Once Juanito got his hands on the little fellow and held him by

one ear, but the calf was anxious to frolic, so he jerked away and kicked up his heels again. Then, abruptly, something happened. Tito saw two big dark eyes looking directly into his small bright ones. The calf was looking mischievously at the tiny brightly clad bandit and was coming directly toward him.

Of course, the little calf didn't mean any harm. He only wanted to play and maybe to touch the brave little fellow with his nose. Juanito saw what was about to happen, but he couldn't get to Tito in time. Kenny saw, too, and tried to catch the calf by the tail, but that did no good. The young animal kept looking straight into Tito's eyes and prancing stubbornly toward him.

Tito clinched his fists. His whiskers bristled furiously. Then—woe, woe, woe—he felt a blunt wet nose against his. He saw a black tongue come out to lick at his paint. And he felt himself shoved backwards, tumbling head over heels down, down, down into the well!

"Now see," Juanito shouted. "See what you've done?"

The little calf only kicked up his heels again and bounded out the gate and down the street.

"What'll we do?" Kenny whispered worriedly. "The water'll spoil him, won't it?"

Juanito was almost crying, but his mind worked fast.

"The bucket," he said. "Maybe we can save him with the bucket."

Juanito's mother came running out of the house.

"What's happened? What's happened?"

The boys told her how the calf had come into the yard, scampered round and round till he was tired and then tried to lick the little bandit's paint off. Yes, and he had pushed Tito backwards into the well.

Señor Pérez had now come to the door in his white pajamalike clothes, a red Indian blanket over his arm. He had heard some of what the others said.

"Well, what are you waiting for?" he called. "Drop the bucket down. See if you can't bring him up before the water spoils the pasteboard."

Juanito let the rope slip through his hands as the bucket went down into the well. Looking over the stone fence, he tried to see the white hat, and the furious whiskers of his tiny bandit on the water far below. There was something, but Juanito couldn't be sure what it was. Perhaps it was just a shiny glint on the face of the water. At any rate, he aimed his bucket as well as he could, let it sink into the water, then began drawing it up to the surface.

Kenny put his hand on the rope and helped him pull. Juanito's father and mother were both standing beside the well now, looking over the low wall.

Suddenly the mother's eye caught sight of a bobbing object in the pail.

"Oh, there he is! Easy, Juanito. Don't shake the bucket. There he is! Easy now. You might splash him out. . . . Now."

She leaned far over the stone railing and snatched the little man from the water.

"Is he spoiled?" Juanito cried. "Is the paint running off? Is the pasteboard soft?"

"The paint's running just a little, but he isn't spoiled, though," his mother said. "Here, let's stand him in the bright sunshine. This flower pot will be a good place. He floated on the water, but he didn't really get wet through and through."

"I'm glad of that," Kenny said sympathetically.

Señor Pérez looked at the little fellow carefully.

"No, he's not quite spoiled," he said. "But that was a close call. Don't stand him on the well-stone any more if you don't want to lose him."

"I won't," Juanito said.

And Tito, having no love of water, was glad to hear him say it. He knew that the little boy meant what he said.

"If Uncle Diego gets in from the country with that load of pottery, come down to the cafe and get me," Señor Pérez said to Juanito.

Then he threw his bright red serape across his shoulder and went out the wide gate into the street. Tito watched him from his place in the flower pot.

"Come with me," Juanito's mother said to the boys. "Let me give you some pennies. I want to send you for some *camotes.*"

"Sweet things," Juanito whispered when he saw Kenny didn't understand.

Both of them were eager to go for her.

25

CHAPTER 4

DRY SOUP

It was afternoon when the man came with the pottery. Tito was still standing in the flower pot on the wall, and Juanito and Kenny were sitting on the well-stone teaching each other words.

"House," Kenny said.

"*Casa,*" Juanito answered.

"Boy."

"*Muchacho.*"

"Thank you."

"*Muchas gracias.*"

Tito wasn't very much interested. He knew what people said no matter what language they spoke. But soon he saw a country fellow standing at the patio gate. He was very dusty, a brown man with loose-fitting clothes and a broad straw sombrero. He wore sandals, and behind him Tito saw the face of a faithful, patient, sad-eyed little burro. A moment later the man swung the gates inward and the little pack animal, heavily loaded, trotted into the courtyard.

The clear afternoon sky made a lovely blue dome over the green patio. Soft big clouds strayed across the sky like great silvery sheep in the meadows of heaven. Both boys rose to greet the newcomer. Kenny didn't know who the man was or what the animal carried in the great straw-lined rope bags that bulged like balloons on either side of the burro's back, but Juanito knew right away.

"Papá's gone to the cafe," he said. "I'll run and get him."

"No hurry," Uncle Diego said. "It will take some time to unload all this pottery. Every piece has to be handled carefully."

Kenny persuaded Juanito to wait till he had seen how the earthen jugs and vases, jars and dishes were packed, then they started toward the gate together. Hearing a new voice in the patio, Juanito's mother came to the door and stood in the archway without speaking. Heavy braids of hair hung down the sides of her face. She had been cooking and she dried her hands on her apron as she watched the man unload the burro.

A cool breeze was beginning to stir. Uncle Diego had said there was no need to hurry, but the two boys began running almost as soon as they were outside the gate. It was easier to run down the hill than to walk. They reached the plaza, crossed a cobble-stone street and entered the cafe where Señor Pérez so often sat with his good friends and talked.

"Papá," Juanito said, "the pottery has come.

28

Uncle Diego's unloading the burro now."

"So soon? Well, now, that uncle of yours is not as sleepy as he looks. I'll be right along."

He raised his glass to finish the soda he was drinking. The boys did not wait but walked along ahead.

When Señor Pérez got home, he showed the boys how to help him place the pottery pieces some in one place and some in another, grouping them according to shape and size in the corner where he did his painting. Both boys helped willingly, and soon the great bags were empty and there was nothing left in them but the straw in which the pottery had been packed.

Uncle Diego went into the house and passed a few words with his sister Carmen, who was Juanito's mother, and then came back to the well and drew a bucket of water for his faithful burro and one for himself. When they had both drunk all they could hold, the quiet country man unfolded his serape and put it over his shoulders by sticking his head through a hole he had cut in the middle.

"There's a cool wind blowing," he said.

"Won't you stay and have a bite to eat, brother?" Juanito's mother called from the doorway, her face perspiring from standing over the charcoal stove in the kitchen.

"No, thank you," he answered. "I must buy some things before the shops close, and then I'll have to start home. My family expects me tonight, and it's a long way to walk. I'll be leaving now."

Señor Pérez paid his brother-in-law for bringing the pottery and stood at the gate waving good-bye as the copper-brown country man and his mouse-gray burro went down the road. Juanito and Kenny were still busy looking at the various pieces of earthenware Uncle

Diego had made and brought to Señor Pérez to be decorated with brightly colored birds and flowers.

Poor little Tito had been blown over by the afternoon breeze and lay on his back in the flower pot, seeing nothing but the great dome of heaven and the fleecy clouds like mammoth sheep.

Señora Carmen was in the door again.

"Well, your food is ready, little men and big man," she said kindly.

Tito almost rolled out of his flower pot. He thought at first she was talking to him. But in a minute he understood better. She was calling the boys little men.

"This is the day you promised to eat dinner with us," Juanito said, turning to Kenny.

"*Gracias*," Kenny said, using his new language easily. "I told my mama and papa you had asked me and they said all right."

They drew some water to wash their faces and hands. Señor Pérez washed out of doors, too. Then all took big drinks of water and went inside to the dining room.

The table was set with two bowls of chili sauce and a large dish filled with a paste of avocados with chopped onions and tomatoes. There was also a big pile of hot tortillas wrapped in a cloth. When they were all seated, Juanito's mother brought in four brown cups full of delicious clear soup, and into these each one squeezed the juice of half a lime he found beside his plate.

Taking her seat, Señora Pérez uncovered the tall pile of thin tortillas and handed a few to each one at the table. On these she spread the avocado paste for Kenny, who didn't seem to understand, and twisted each one into a tight little roll with the delicious green paste running out of each end.

The next course (for even the poor people in Mexico serve each item of food separately) Juanito's family called *sopa seca* or dry soup. This consisted of a big platter of tender dry rice colored with red from tomato sauce and chili. It had been prepared in such a manner as to make each grain stand out from the others, and Kenny thought this one of the finest dishes he had ever eaten.

"Dry soup, you call it?" he asked.

"Yes, *sopa seca*," Juanito answered.

The others smiled. It did sound a little funny.

"What kind of egg will you have on your soup?" the mother asked Kenny.

"Fried," the boy said.

The others chose to have theirs fried, too, so Señora Pérez left them a few moments while she prepared the eggs over her charcoal stove in the little adjoining kitchen.

Guisado followed, a meat stew highly seasoned with chili peppers, which, like much of the other food, burned Kenny's mouth. The tortilla was used as a spoon in eating this, but since Kenny had a hard time, Señora Pérez got him a fork. While she was up, she brought in the salad, chopped lettuce with a radish nearly a foot long lying across the plate.

They ate quietly, and Juanito knew why Kenny's eyes got large when the mother brought in the *verdura*, the green vegetable which today consisted of squash cooked with carrots. She smeared more avocado paste on another tortilla for him, and rolled it up. Kenny ate

31

it all, but his eyes did get big. He was wondering how he could ever hold so much.

"Does the chili burn your mouth?" Señor Pérez asked, smiling as he saw Kenny reach for the water.

"Just a little," Kenny said.

"Wait a minute. I'll get you something sweet and cool for that," the man said.

The father went out the front door. When he returned in a few moments, he was carrying a large wide-mouthed jug filled with ice-cold pineapple juice. He got pottery mugs from a cupboard, filled them one by one, and placed them beside the plates. Kenny drank all of his at once, and Señor Pérez refilled it promptly.

Kenny thought he had never eaten so much in his life, but the food was so good he didn't want to stop—even though the chili peppers were hot.

Señora Pérez cleared away their plates, went into the kitchen again and returned with a large earthen pot of beans that had been simmering on the charcoal stove a long time and was all blackened on the bottom. She set it on a red straw mat and began serving all the plates very generously. She took a spoon and dipped chili sauce for every plate except Kenny's. She could see that some of the food had been burning him so she decided he had perhaps eaten enough chili for one day. It didn't seem hot to them; they were used to it.

The fruit followed, mangoes, oranges, pomegranates, and figs. Kenny looked at the heaping basket and decided he'd try a mango, since he had never tasted one before. He was full, but he was sure it was a good fruit.

He was so full he had no taste for the dessert, which was guava jelly served in large squares. It seemed to him too sweet. But he tried to eat a little to keep the others company. He couldn't understand how Juanito's mother and father could take coffee, too, after eating so heartily for about an hour and a half.

"I think I should go home now," he said to them, drowsily.

"Already?" Juanito said.

"Stay for supper," said the mother. "We'll have enchiladas and chocolate tonight."

"I'd like to, but I'm afraid mama and papa—"

"Well, *mañana*, maybe? Perhaps some other day?"

Kenny smiled, going out the door into the courtyard. He was so full that when he walked he waddled.

In his flower pot, neglected and forgotten, Tito heard the gate swing, shivered in the cool afternoon breeze and wondered if he was to be neglected the rest of the day. Would Juanito leave him out in the evening dew to get his paint all spoiled, his pasteboard softened? Oh, there were so many things for a little figure of a bandit to worry about. His rabbit whiskers bristled furiously. He clinched his fists— and just lay there.

CHAPTER 5

LOCKED IN A MINE

The next day the boys watched Señor Pérez paint lovely birds and flowers on some of his pottery in the corner of the courtyard. After a while Kenny persuaded Juanito to come to his house, and it was then they remembered Tito, whom they had left in the flower pot the previous afternoon.

As a result of his fall into the well, the little fellow had been badly damaged. Spending the night in the flower pot and being wet by the dew perhaps did him no good either. At any rate, he was now a sorrowful sight. His paint had run. His little blue coat had faded. His bright red girdle had disappeared. He had lost all the white buttons on the sides of his pants. His dashing white sombrero was now as brown and ugly as a gunny sack. His cheeks were as pale as chalk and tears had run out of his eyes, streaking his face.

Nothing had happened to his furious little beard, however; the thatch of hair above his forehead was as bushy as usual, and his tiny brave fist was still clinched and raised indignantly. Yet Tito was a pitiful sight. Juanito felt sorry for him. It made his heart tender to see the little fellow so marred.

"Poor Tito," he said to Kenny, holding the small papier-mâché figure in the palm of his hand.

"He's still well and strong," Kenny said, "even if his paint is spoiled."

"Yes, but he doesn't feel the same. You see, Tito loves bright clothes. He's proud."

"If he were a doll, you could have your mama make him some new things."

"I wouldn't have him if he were a doll," Juanito said petulantly. "He'd belong to some girl, and she could look after him the best way she could. But Tito's a regular fellow."

"Bring him along," Kenny said.

They left the patio in the bright morning sunshine, went out the gate and started down the road toward the red house that was neither small nor large. Tito's heart thumped. He was a great one for going places. Every time Juanito went out the gate, he began to feel excited.

Kenny's mother and father, Mr. and Mrs. Strange, were not at home. Concha, the Indian woman who kept the house clean for them, said they had gone up on one of the higher peaks above the town. They had worn their buff-colored smocks and navy blue berets and carried their easels, so she supposed they had gone to paint.

"We can find them," Kenny said. "Let's go too."

Juanito was willing and Tito was more than pleased.

After a long walk on a winding path, they reached a high point and saw the two artists working at their easels on a twin peak that was not more than a block away. Kenny called to them cheerfully and both stopped and waved their brushes. The boys reached their hill and saw what they were painting.

Down below the town of Taxco looked magical. The red clay tops of houses, the little green patios with wells or fountains in the centers and yellow flowers growing, scarcely seemed real. In the center was the plaza, dense with trees and deep green. In front of it stood the cathedral, very tall, very grand. Around the plaza were shops and booths, most of them ornamented with crepe tissue paper and paper cut-outs. . . . And this was the picture each of the artists was painting on his canvas.

"What are those piles of dirt over there?" Kenny said to Juanito after a while.

The Indian youngster turned to see where he was pointing.

"Oh, mines," he said. "Old silver mines, no more good. Want to see them?"

Kenny said that he did.

"Be careful," said the mother, squeezing a little dab of paint out of a tube.

"I say as much. Don't get lost," the father said without looking up from his work.

The boys went down a slope, pausing now and again to pull at leaves or to throw stones. The mines were further away than they had seemed from the peak where Blyth and Myrna Strange were painting.

The boys examined two or three of the old abandoned shafts, venturing inside a few feet, peeping cautiously to see what was back in the black holes, then came to one where a great beam ran across the entrance, supporting some other boards overhead.

"I wonder what's back inside," Kenny said, pulling a big loose stone out from underneath the beam.

"Let's find out," Juanito suggested.

Tito quaked with fear. What kind of black hole was this that they wanted to enter? What might happen to a little pasteboard man in such a dismal shaft? Were there animals back there, badgers, wild cats? Oh, it was a fearful moment for Tito. He was brave enough for his size, but, you know, that wasn't much. And Tito had just suffered a bad accident the day before, so you couldn't blame him for being quite nervous—if you didn't want to call him really scared.

"What about Tito?" Kenny asked.

"He does look scared, doesn't he?"

"I'll say he does. Is he trembling or is that the wind blowing his whiskers?"

Both of them laughed.

"I'll just stand him here on this rock," Juanito said. "If I dropped him back in the dark, I might not ever find him. We might step on him and mash him up."

"Yes," Kenny said.

"This stone is a good place for him. He can be a look-out for us. There, stand there, little bandit."

Tito was happy. It made him proud to be stood at the entrance of the mine shaft and given such an important job. He made up his mind to do the best he could, even if he was a pretty wretched sight with all his gay clothes ruined, his painted eyes running.

"Watch out for us," Juanito said.

They left the little bandit and started back into the black hole in the mountain side. Back, back, back they went. It was terribly dark. It was quiet and still. The walls were damp, and now and again a bit of gravel fell. Occasionally a drop of water splashed on a stone. Once Kenny looked back. The entrance seemed a long way off, but it was easy to see though it looked small now. Ahead—blackness. This was going to be a real adventure. On they went.

Outside on his stone little Tito kept guard. The afternoon sun moved steadily across the sky and began slipping down toward the rim of the earth, behind the beautiful line of hills. Why were the boys staying so long, Tito wondered. Time was passing. Didn't they know that? Tito was beginning to feel worried when suddenly he heard an awful jolt at the entrance to the mine.

Dear, dear, dear! What could that be? Tito could have cried for fear. His little painted eyes were not so good, but now he could just dimly see that the great beam had suddenly fallen across the door of the mine. Some of the boards had fallen, too, and some of the rocks and dirt, and the entrance was barred. Juanito and Kenny were inside!

Tito was so distressed he wanted to tear his hair. Something horrible had happened, but what could a little pasteboard bandit do? The boys had told him to be look-out, but how could he help now? How were the boys ever going to get out of that black hole with such a heavy beam across the entrance? Oh, woe! woe! woe! thought Tito. He clinched his tiny fists; his whiskers bristled. If he could only move! Run for help! Shout and call!

CHAPTER 6

TITO BECOMES A HERO

Blyth and Myrna Strange finished their painting and folded their easels. It was getting late, and they were sure Concha would be waiting with supper for them. Where were the boys, Kenny and Juanito? Where was that little bandit, Tito?

"Kenny should know better than to wander so far away and stay so long," Blyth Strange said, wrinkling his forehead.

"I'm getting worried," Myrna added, looking far across the hillside.

They waited a little longer, searching with their eyes for their son and his little Mexican companion.

Neither of them had entirely completed the picture on which he was working, but on each canvas, from slightly different angles, there was a fine reproduction of the little town viewed from the hill. Each had caught the vivid warm colors of the houses; the brick-red roofs, the patches of cucumber green, the gray cobble-stones, and pumpkin-colored walls were all there.

"Well, we can't go home without Kenny," Mr. Strange said. "And that little friend of his—why Juanito's mother and father will feel terrible if we don't send him home soon."

"What shall we do, Blyth?"

"Stay here," he said to his wife. "Keep these things. I'll go look for them."

Myrna kept looking across the hillside at the old abandoned mines in the distance and at the heaps of slag piled near the openings of the holes. After a while she began shaking her head slowly.

"No," she told him. "I'm going, too. These painting things will be safe here. I'm worried about Kenny. I'm going, too."

"Well," Blyth said slowly. "All right."

They went down one slope and up another. They crossed a level place and crept along a high ledge. They

42

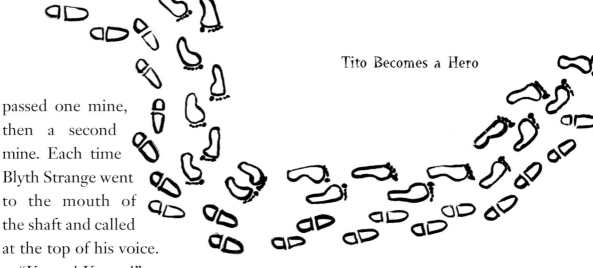

passed one mine, then a second mine. Each time Blyth Strange went to the mouth of the shaft and called at the top of his voice.

"Kenny! Kenny!"

There was an echo of his words deep in the heart of the earth, but no answer came. Surely Kenny was not back in one of those dangerous holes, they told each other. Surely he and Juanito knew better than to do such a thing. But, just to be quite sure, they thought it would do no harm to call. Blyth Strange called, and then his wife, Myrna, called.

"Kenny! Kenny!"

The second shaft was just like the first. He was not in it either. There were footprints where the boys had come to the entrances and peeped in, one little barefoot boy and one with New York shoes, but there were also prints showing that they had come back to the path again and continued up the hill.

The sun was quite out of sight now and the sky was a soft bandanna handkerchief of rose and gold. It was past supper time and they knew Concha was waiting to put the food on the table, but where was Kenny? Where was his little friend, Juanito?

Presently they came to a third mine. Their hearts began to beat rapidly. They were so excited and troubled by now that at first neither of them noticed a little pasteboard fellow standing on a stone, clinching his tiny fists.

"What!" Mr. Strange said. "Isn't this that little toy Juanito showed us?"

"Why yes," his wife said. "Oh, dear, he must have gotten wet. His paint is all spoiled. But what does this mean?"

Her husband caught sight of the heavy beam that had fallen across the entrance to the mine. He wrinkled his forehead and looked at the other boards that had fallen, too, partly covered with loose earth.

"It means that our Kenny is in that horrible hole," he said. "It means that he and Juanito left this little fellow here while they went inside to explore. And it means that that beam has fallen and locked them inside!"

"Oh, no, no!" Mrs. Strange began to cry softly. "What shall we do? Do you think they're hurt, Blyth?"

"We'll have to be calm," her husband said, throwing off his smock and going to work furiously.

Tito began to feel better. He wondered if he had done his work well, just standing there on guard. Had he not shown the mother and father of Kenny where the boys were? But the main question now was whether or not the boys were hurt and how they would get them out.

Mrs. Strange climbed up on a heap of dirt that had fallen with the beam and called through an opening above.

"Kenny! Oh, Kenny!"

Her husband stopped tugging at the beam and listened.

Tito listened, too, straining his little pasteboard ears.

Then, very faintly, he heard something. It said, "Mother! Mother!"

Blyth Strange found that he could not make much headway trying to move the big beam. He would have to remove the fallen dirt and rocks first. His wife helped him. It was hard work, and they began to perspire. But Kenny was inside. And with him was Juanito. A shovel would have made things easier, but they had none and they couldn't wait to get one. The sun was gone, and it was getting darker and darker.

Finally, with great effort, Mr. Strange began to move the heavy beam. He had cleared a way that enabled him to drag the thing two or three feet. Then he put his head in the new opening and called, "Kenny! Kenny!"

Tito listened for the answer with all his ears.

"Yes, Daddy," Kenny's voice said. "We're right here. I think we can get through."

They came wriggling out of the dark, first Kenny and then Juanito. The mother and father were so happy to see them that they forgot to scold the boys for what they had done. Instead, Myrna Strange said, "Hurry, both of you. Juanito's mother and father will be wondering where he is, and Concha is waiting with supper for us. It'll be dark and we won't be able to find our painting things. Hurry, both of you."

"That's true," her husband said, "but we don't want to forget Tito, do we?"

They all turned around at once, for there was the tiny fellow about to be left on his stone.

"No, indeed," Myrna Strange said. "Tito saved you naughty

boys! He stood on that rock and let us know where you were. We couldn't leave Tito. Here, take good care of him, Juanito."

"Thank you, I will," Juanito said.

Tito's little chest nearly burst with pride. It was the biggest moment of his life. Perhaps, he thought, as they hurried down the mountains in the dusk, he had saved Juanito and his little friend from starving to death locked in that horrible mining shaft. He had been on guard and had pointed the way for the rescuers.

CHAPTER 7

COUSINS FROM THE COUNTRY

Tito was standing in his flower pot again. High on the side of the patio wall he felt the cool December breeze blowing through his bushy whiskers and through his thatch of rebellious rabbit hair. Poor Tito's eyes were not so good now. Most of the paint had run down the sides of his face and he could scarcely see. His little painted coat, his girdle and shirt, his pants with the white buttons were getting worse and worse, too.

Yet the little fellow was not unhappy. Juanito and Kenny came and spoke to him affectionately almost every day. They would never forget how he had saved them from that mine by standing guard and letting Mr. and Mrs. Strange know where the boys were. Tito always liked to have people praise him, especially Juanito and Kenny, whom he loved.

In the courtyard Señor Pérez worked faithfully at his decorating. Christmas was not far away, and he wanted to get a good amount of pottery painted so that he might sell it and have money to invite his friends to his house for a celebration of the holidays.

One day Juanito came through the gate from the street and stood watching his father work for a long time. Tito watched too, but his eyes were dim. The father painted in silence. Finally he finished the bowl on which he was working and stood up to stretch the kink out of his back.

"Well, Juanito, what's my young man thinking about?"

The boy paused a moment before he answered. Then he said, "Tito's clothes are bad, papá. His eyes are almost washed out."

"Well, now, I'm not a tailor, son," the man said smiling. "And Tito is not exactly a doll."

Juanito put his hands in his pockets, thinking. A bird circled over the patio, perched on the corner of the stone wall near a spot where the plaster was falling, then flew away. A barefoot country man passed the gate with a huge pile of chicken coops on his back, all of them tied together and a chicken in each one. He called, *"Gallinas, pollos, pollitos!"* A woman passed, going the other way, with a wide round basket of fruit on her head: pomegranates, oranges, limes, melons, and bananas neatly piled on shiny greens to make them look pretty.

Juanito waited till she had passed before he spoke again to his father. "Couldn't you paint Tito some new eyes and another coat and girdle and put some more buttons on his pants?"

"That's an idea," Señor Pérez said, turning. "Where is he? We'll dress him up for Christmas."

49

Juanito went to the wall, climbed up on a stone that jutted out and took the little bandit from his high flower pot.

Señor Pérez examined the small cardboard figure carefully, turning it over and over in his hand.

"Wouldn't you rather have me buy you a new toy?" he asked.

"No," Juanito said promptly. "I'd rather have you paint Tito some new clothes."

"Well, if that's your wish—of course, I haven't much time. But run along and play and meanwhile I'll see what I can do."

Juanito went to play with Kenny. They wandered through the town and found an old house that had grass growing in the cracks of the stones and at the corners of the roof. It was so old it had hardly any plaster left, but the house was still strong and the stone walls looked as if they would stand a good many more generations.

When they returned to Juanito's house late in the afternoon, they found Mr. and Mrs. Strange visiting in the courtyard, talking to Señor Pérez and watching him work. Tito was drying in the sun, dressed in new painted things from head to foot. He felt like a new person. His bright new eyes were round and shining, and he was finer looking than ever.

"Did you have a good walk?" Mrs. Strange said as the boys came through the gate.

"Yes, fine," Kenny told her. "Look at Tito."

"He is dressed up for Christmas," Juanito cried happily. "My papá, he did it. Look at Tito now—my banditito!"

Mr. and Mrs. Strange came and inspected him.

"Isn't he darling," said Mrs. Strange. "Just see how he stands there under that geranium. Wouldn't he make a cute picture, though? I

50

think I'd like to paint him, Blyth, just as he is there, bright and brave."

Tito's little pasteboard chest filled with pride. Did this American lady mean she wanted to paint his picture? The picture of little Tito?

"He fell in the well and spoiled his clothes," said Señor Pérez, "so Juanito persuaded me to make him some new ones."

"We saw him before," Mr. Strange said. "But he did not look nearly so fine as he does now."

"May I take him home in that flower pot and paint him standing there under the geranium?" Mrs. Strange asked Juanito. "I'll take good care of him."

Juanito smiled and said yes.

"Thanks, so much. I'll borrow him after Christmas—and paint him life size, as big as a real man."

That was almost too much for Tito. He reeled, and nearly tumbled out of the flower pot. Life size! Like a real man! A picture of Tito by an artist! It was certainly worth waiting for to have this happen to you.

The afternoon passed and the Strange family had to be going home. Before they went, however, Señora Pérez left her cooking, came to the door wiping her hands on her apron and asked if the whole family would not come to celebrate Christmas with them. There would be Uncle Diego's family from the country, too, and they would break piñatas every night for nine nights at their *posadas*.

Mr. and Mrs. Strange and Kenny did not know what a piñata was, but all of them were eager to come to the Christmas fun, and to find out.

"We'd love to accept," said Mrs. Strange, standing at the gate.

"We'll expect you then," Juanito's mother said.

When the visitors left, it was time to lock the gate and go in to supper. Señor Pérez pulled the gates together and fastened them with a strong chain, as he always did at night, then put a prop against them for extra protection. Juanito took Tito down carefully and carried him into the house.

At the supper table the family talked about nothing but Christmas. Even Tito became excited and began to feel that he couldn't wait for the holidays to come.

"Never mind," Señor Pérez said to Juanito. "You will have to be patient. The *posadas* are still a week off."

But three nights later, when the gates were locked and propped, when the family was at the supper table eating enchiladas, Juanito heard a great banging beyond the patio and the voices of many children calling him.

Everybody got up and hurried through the courtyard.

"Hello," the voices called. "Hello, Juanito. Hello, Uncle Juan. Hello, Aunt Carmen. Hello, little Juan. Hello. Hello."

They unhooked the gates and let them swing open. There in the blue twilight stood Uncle Diego beside his faithful burro; with him were Aunt María, Grandma Lupe and Juanito's five cousins, Luana, Angelina, Carlos, Aurora and baby Paco, whom they often called Paquito. They had all made a long journey, but they were laughing and cheerful. They had come to visit their relatives in town and to stay till after Christmas.

"*Qué milagro! Qué milagro!* How wonderful," Señora Carmen kept saying.

The little crowd swept through the patio gate and filled the courtyard with the music of their voices and their laughter.

Little Tito, standing on the shelf in Juanito's room and hearing all the excitement, thought that Christmas had started already. Tito didn't know much about things like that, but he was happy, too.

CHAPTER 8

NINE DAYS CHRISTMAS

Juanito's mother told Kenny that there would be nine days of Christmas parties. She called them *posadas*. They would be held at the different houses of their friends, and the last one would be at Juanito's house on Christmas Eve. Kenny must be sure to come, he and his mother and father, she explained.

So the night before Christmas, Blyth and Myrna Strange and their son left their little red house that was neither large nor small and went out into the cool Mexican evening and up the rocky little streets of Taxco until they came to the Pérez home, where the soft sound of Christmas carols came floating out the gate to meet them. The Pérez family and all the children and the guests and their children were marching slowly around the courtyard, singing about the first Christmas in their high clear Indian voices.

"How beautiful!" said Myrna Strange, stopping at the entrance to the courtyard. Blyth Strange and Kenny stopped, too. The singers did not see them until they had finished their song.

Juanito saw them first and came running over to greet them. His father and mother followed him. And then all of Juanito's little cousins came to welcome the Americans who had come to their party. They were led into the courtyard and introduced to everybody.

There were dark young men, and lovely young brown girls in soft, bright-colored dresses, and old ladies, some in black silk waists with high collars, black shawls thrown about their shoulders or over their heads. There was a nice old man with a leather-brown face and a very white beard. Almost all of the grown-up guests had on shoes, but some wore sandals, and most of the children were barefooted, dancing happily about the patio.

But what most attracted Kenny's attention, and indeed that of his mother and father, too, was the large life-size figure of a jolly Mexican-doll character named Mamerto copied from the funny papers, a gay fat fellow here made of cardboard and tissue paper with a huge potlike stomach and enormous mustaches under his wide sombrero. An enormous doll, he was swinging overhead from a rope strung across the patio.

Juanito explained to Kenny why his stomach was so big— because it was made of a big round pottery jar, that was why, covered with a tissue paper shirt. And it was filled with good things, that stomach, gifts and fruits and nuts for children, so Juanito had told him. Later in the evening it would be broken.

"How do you like our piñata?" Señor Pérez asked.

Kenny was too interested to say a word, but his mother answered, "Why, I've never seen anything like it! It's the jolliest doll I've ever seen. But tell me, why is it hung so high up that nobody can reach it?"

"Wait," said Señor Pérez. "You will see."

Just then Uncle Diego, who had brought his guitar in with him from the country, began to play and sing. He sang a very long half-gay half-sad song with a great many verses, and everybody joined in the choruses, even little Juanito.

They sang several songs, and after that one of the little girls from the country recited a poem about selling flowers in the market place. Juanito said a poem, too. And then everybody began to call on the Americans to do something.

"Say your little verse for them, son," Blyth Strange told Kenny, "the funny one about the cow."

"It's not in Spanish," Kenny explained, but everyone said that made no difference. So he stood up and recited:

> I never saw a purple cow,
> I never hope to see one,
> But I can tell you, anyhow,
> I'd rather see than be one.

Everybody applauded and laughed as Kenny bowed. Then Blyth

Strange borrowed Uncle Diego's guitar and began to play and sing:

Oh, Susanna,
Don't you cry for me,
'Cause I'm going out to Oregon
With my banjo on my knee.

Then he and Myrna Strange sang together the old American song called "Listen to the Mocking Bird," which all the people at the party liked very much even if they didn't understand the words.

But it was getting late now and the children were all anxious to break the piñata, to see what was hidden inside the stomach of this gay fat fellow swinging in the evening breeze there in the center of the patio, his tissue paper arms waving, his blue legs dangling and blowing in the wind.

Kenny wondered how this ceremony that Juanito had told him so much about was to take place, but he did not have to wonder long. Amidst much laughing and joking, the chairs were moved back and plenty of room made in the center of the patio.

"Who wants to be the first to break the piñata?" Señor Pérez asked, as the guests grouped themselves against the wall.

"I do," said a tall young man stepping up. But everybody said no, he would never do! He was too tall, he could almost reach the piñata and pull it down.

Señor Pérez had a big white

58

handkerchief in his hands, and when the first person was finally selected, a little girl named Luz, he put the handkerchief around her head and blindfolded her so that she couldn't see anything. Then he gave her the long pole that they used to prop the door shut every night.

"She must try to break the piñata with the stick while she is blindfolded," Señor Pérez explained to Blyth and Myrna Strange. "It's lots of fun watching people try to find Mamerto blindfolded."

Juanito and his cousins took the little girl by the arms and led her beneath the swinging figure, so that she could touch it with the pole when she waved it above her head.

"You see where Mamerto is?" they asked the little girl, laughing.

"I feel him," she said, poking him gently with the stick.

"Then find him again and try to break him open," they said slyly as they led her away toward a corner of the courtyard. There they turned her around and around until she didn't know what direction she was facing when they stopped. Then they just left her standing there blindfolded with the long stick in her hands.

"Try and find Mamerto now," everybody teased and laughed. "Where is he?"

"Here I come," said the little girl, as she advanced haltingly, step by step, waving the pole. But the funny thing was that she wasn't going toward the piñata at all. She was walking blindly right toward the people grouped near the sides of the house. Everybody scattered laughing.

"Watch out, or she'll drop the pole on you," everybody cried.

"Run, Kenny," Juanito yelled, laughing, "or she'll bring the stick down on your head."

The little girl, realizing she was going the wrong way, turned and went in another direction, walking slowly and waving her stick in the air, trying to find the tantalizing hanging figure that she wanted to break open.

"You're getting warm," somebody cried.

"There he is now, hit him," yelled Juanito.

The little girl brought her pole swishing through the air—but she didn't hit a thing! She was two or three yards away from the piñata, so everybody roared with laughter. She laughed too. And after one or two more trials, she gave up. When Señor Pérez untied the blindfold, she found that she had wandered way over by the well, and was nowhere near the gay funny little man whose clay shell of a stomach was full of gifts.

But she was good-natured about it and didn't mind that every-one laughed loudly.

The next to try his luck was a young cousin of Juanito's named Carlos. Once blindfolded, Carlos dashed madly toward what he thought was the piñata, and brought his stick slicing

through the air with full force. But what he hit neither cracked, nor broke nor moved. He hit the wall!

Everyone screamed with laughter as he tore the bandage from his eyes to discover that he was standing with his back to the swinging doll and his face to the wall.

"Let Kenny try," everyone said.

"Yes," said Juanito and his father both at once. "Let Kenny have a chance at it."

So they blindfolded Kenny, gave him the long pole, and turned him around and around near the gate. Then they left him to find his way toward the piñata as best he could.

"Watch out! You'll fall in the well!" his father called, but Kenny knew Blyth Strange was only teasing him.

"You're near," Juanito yelled when Kenny kept getting farther and farther away.

"No, you're not," a little girl cried. "Don't believe Juanito."

Kenny was not sure which way to turn, but he kept searching step by step, his eyes blindfolded and his stick waving above his head.

People kept screaming and laughing and teasing. But Kenny noticed now that everyone was really excited, and shouting more than ever.

"You're warm!"

"You're near him!"

"Now, hit it!"

Kenny struck once blindly with the long stick. An excited scream went up. He realized that he had not missed the stuffed little man

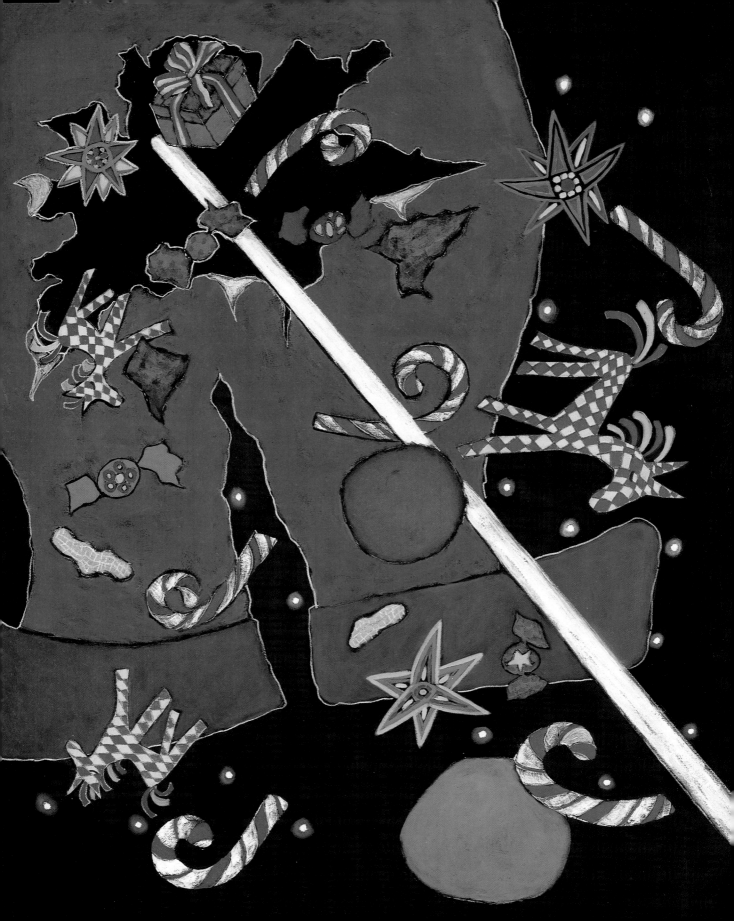

by much. He swung again. This time he felt the stick strike a tissue paper leg. He heard the paper tear, as everyone laughed and screamed in excitement.

"If I could only see," thought Kenny, "I'd split that piñata wide open. But I'm almost sure I'll hit it this time anyway."

He took the pole in both hands, leaned back with it raised above his head, and struck a furious blow through the air. And sure enough, he hit Mamerto squarely in the stomach! The swinging doll's fat clay girth broke into a hundred pieces, and all the gifts and fruits, candies and nuts, fell into the patio amidst the delighted shrieks of the onlookers.

Kenny tore off his blindfold just in time to see all the youngsters scrambling on the stone floor for the prizes that had fallen to earth.

Kenny began to scramble, too, on his hands and knees. Everybody was good-natured, laughing, and polite about it. And several children ran to their parents, or older brothers and sisters, to offer them handfuls of peanuts they had picked up, or an apple, or an orange; or to give them a little straw-horse to hold, or some other simple gift that had fallen from the now broken body of the piñata.

Kenny gave his mother a handful of candy and nuts he had gathered. And to his father he gave several pieces of sugarcane.

"Wasn't I lucky to be the one to break the piñata?" he asked proudly.

"You certainly were," said Blyth Strange. "How could you find it?"

"I couldn't see him," said Kenny, "but I felt him with the stick."

"I wouldn't say you *felt* him," said his father. "I'd say you socked him one."

Kenny laughed as he looked up at the cardboard head with the few strands of paper left hanging from it, that had once been Mamerto's body. On the ground lay the bits of cracked clay that had been his round fat stomach full of Christmas cheer.

The grown-ups were being served cakes and wine and pineapple juice now while the children still scampered about picking up peanuts or cuts of sugarcane that might have rolled into cracks and corners of the courtyard. But shortly it was time for the party to break up, and everyone began to say goodnight.

"What a delightful Christmas Eve," Myrna Strange said, as they went down the starlit street toward their house that was neither large nor small.

"Yes," her husband answered, "very jolly, indeed."

"A piñata's almost as good as a Christmas tree," Kenny said sleepily, "except that it hasn't got candles."

CHAPTER 9

ALL THE TOYS MARCH

Juanito saw that things were not the same, but he couldn't imagine what had made the change. He was still lying on the floor where he had fallen asleep, but the other people had left the patio, and for some reason the courtyard was brighter than at midday. Something was wrong with Tito, too. He didn't look the same.

In a moment Juanito realized what the change had been. The little bandit was not clinching his fist in the air. He had his hands in his pockets, in fact! And as Juanito stared at him he began to smile behind his bushy rabbit-hair whiskers. For the first time Juanito saw his teeth.

Then—more astonishing still—he heard the little pasteboard fellow's voice. Tito spoke!

He said, "You're asleep, Juanito."

"Yes," Juanito answered. "People stayed so long and we played so hard I couldn't keep my eyes open any longer."

"I know. You were tired. It's a fine Christmas, though."

Just then another strange little voice spoke in the corner of the patio.

"You're right, Tito. I never thought it would be so grand."

Juanito looked up and saw a straw horse trotting across the courtyard with a little straw rider bouncing in his saddle. The rider swung himself to the ground and hooked his arm in the horse's bridle. He and Tito shook hands and laughed together. Juanito gave them each a handful of peanuts.

Now that the visitors were all gone, he thought he might just as well get his playthings together, so he began to walk around the well. Where was his new bank—the monkey on top of the cucumber?

He found the cucumber in a corner where one of his cousins had dropped it, but the monkey was gone. Juanito almost cried. Somebody must have broken the clay monkey off the cucumber bank.

"Don't worry," a gay voice called from a flower pot. "I'm all right, Juanito." And sure enough, there on the wall was the little brown monkey with his red cap.

"Well, don't forget where you belong," Juanito said, much relieved. "You're the most important part of the bank."

"I won't," the tiny monkey said. "But it is tiresome just sitting on a cucumber all the time."

"Oh, I don't mind if you run and play," Juanito said politely, "only I don't want to lose you."

Two or three pasteboard men who had fallen behind a chair got up and began brushing the dirt from their bright clothes.

"I wish there was something *we* could do," one of them said.

"Why not march around the well," Juanito suggested, "everybody."

The suggestion seemed to please them. Tito, and the straw rider of the straw horse and the monkey, came around and joined the others. A painted pig, very fat and funny, came waddling and grunting as fast as he could travel.

"I'm the leader," Juanito said. "Follow me."

All of them sang as they marched round and round the well, making fancy turns and figure eights. And just then Juanito noticed his father and mother in the doorway of the house, their backs against the light. Uncle Diego and all the youngsters were standing behind them smiling. Evidently they thought the parade was very amusing, for several times they laughed aloud. Then Juanito noticed his mother saying something, so he paused to hear what she said.

For some reason she did not mention the parade at all. Instead she said, "Poor child. He's so tired."

"Yes, he's had too much Christmas," his father said, looking down.

He came over and took Juanito in his arms, and the little fellow began to realize that his eyes were heavy and the patio was dark. "Perhaps," he thought, "perhaps I'm falling asleep!" Was that it? Or was he just waking up a little? Anyway, he was happy in his father's arms.

The man took him into the bedroom and in a few minutes Juanito was tucked under the covers, smiling.

"He must be dreaming," his mother said, as she kissed him good-night and closed the door.

CHAPTER 10

SHOOTING IN THE PLAZA

Another handful of days passed and many things happened.

Everywhere Kenny and Juanito walked in the village there were people selling flowers, baskets of orchids, handfuls of roses, armfuls of lilies, cart loads of pinks.

"It must be spring," Kenny said.

"Yes, nearly," Juanito answered. "But here we have flowers all the year round anyway."

A man came through the streets driving a flock of turkeys. The fowls were so glossy, their heads so red, they seemed to have been enameled.

The turkeys trotted along tamely, a big herd of them, guided by the old man with a long stick.

Men sold ice cream in the street, rolling their small white wagons over the cobblestone roads; and almost every day the two boys got pennies from their fathers and bought little cones in front of the cathedral. Kenny was delighted because there were many new flavors like mamey, tamarind, and melon that he had never tasted before.

Some days they bought *buñuelos* instead, large wafflelike cakes with powdered sugar sprinkled over the top. They were more than a foot across, but when Kenny started eating them he found that they were just crust expanded by air and not really so big as they seemed.

"What is the next holiday?" Kenny asked.

"Easter," Juanito told him. "You'll like it. Easter is fun. Firecrackers and everything."

"I'll be glad of that. I've been feeling lonesome."

"That's because Tito's not here. He's so busy having his picture painted."

They both laughed. They did miss Tito from the patio. But, of course, it was fine to know he was being so highly honored by Kenny's parents.

Then a few days later some workers began suspending lights from tree to tree in the plaza. Shopkeepers began hanging out new decorations. Long paper streamers were tacked to the walls. Other people erected new booths on the square and on the side streets of the village. Some brought little charcoal stoves and set up food stands, stretching blankets overhead to protect themselves against the sun. Things were preparing to happen.

Here and there a firecracker popped. Many of the booths offered a variety of fireworks for sale, Roman candles, sparklers, giant crackers and the like. Some youngsters couldn't wait for the fiesta and lit a few of theirs ahead of time, but mostly the people were waiting for the Saturday before Easter to shoot off their fireworks.

On Good Friday the town became quiet. A steady stream of people went in and out of the cathedral. The next day the celebration became noisy.

Blyth and Myrna Strange left their painting for a few hours and came down the hillside to see the excitement. Kenny and Juanito met them in their smocks and berets walking arm in arm and seeming to enjoy the spectacle greatly. Then the boys lost the couple in the crowd. At another time they saw Señor Pérez and his wife entering the cathedral. But they did not follow this pair either because of the crowds.

The air was burdened with the odors of foods frying or steaming or boiling on little charcoal stoves: *buñuelos*, tacos, tamales, enchiladas. Candy lay in pretty displays on counter after counter in the open air: fudge, taffy and candied fruits—oranges, sweet limes, sliced pineapple, pears. And now more and more children were lighting little firecrackers.

Kenny and Juanito walked till their legs were tired.

"They're going to burn Judases pretty soon," Juanito said.

"What's that like?"

"Well, they're pasteboard Judases they burn. Something like Tito only big as a real man, with lots of different shapes, sometimes a cowboy, sometimes a clown, or a fat man, or a lady, all covered with firecrackers. They hang them up in the trees or in front of the shops and light the firecrackers, and they all go off and the Judas is burnt up."

"We'll see that, won't we?"

"Yes, by and by."

They walked around the plaza again, when suddenly they heard a loud burst of explosions, a whole series of explosions right in front of them. Boom-boom-boom-boom-boom-boom! A cloud of smoke arose amidst the trees and people started suddenly to run in all directions. The noise was just on the other side of the square. What could it be, so sudden and so loud?

The boys were both frightened. Where were their mothers and fathers now? Hadn't they better start toward home? People were running every which way. Someone knocked over a basket of fruit. A young woman spilled a pail of pineapple juice that she had been selling. An old man bumped into a counter and tipped over a tray of candied pumpkin. Everybody was running.

"Are they burning Judas?" Kenny asked as he ran.

"No, no," Juanito answered. "I don't know what this is. It sounds like trouble! Like a revolution! Shooting is dangerous. We'd better get home."

Down the street they went. At the first corner they turned and dashed up a hill to a narrow cobblestone lane. Down a block and then up again. Still they could hear that frightful boom-boom-boom-boom, a great roaring and crackling, like a war. They were both out of breath when they reached Juanito's house and sat down to rest in the patio.

Señor Pérez and his wife came home about an hour later.

"Didn't you boys see them burn Judas?" Juanito's mother said.

The youngsters shook their heads.

"We left when the shooting began," Kenny said. "We didn't want to get hurt."

"The shooting!" Señor Pérez said as the two older people began laughing. "That's good! So you thought it was shooting, did you?"

"What was it?" Juanito asked.

His father was laughing so hard he couldn't explain. Señora Pérez had to tell them what had happened to cause the excitement. A fire-cracker booth had caught on fire and all the giant crackers and little crackers and Roman candles and fire-wheels had all gone off at once, causing a great commotion in the plaza. Nobody was hurt, but a good many other people had evidently thought it was shooting, too, but perhaps they had not run so far before they learned their mistake.

"That's too bad," Kenny said.

"Why?"

"Well, we didn't get to see them burn Judas."

"No," Señor Pérez said, still laughing. "But you heard the shooting. Isn't that enough for one day?"

"We heard it running," Juanito said.

CHAPTER 11

SERENADE

The fiesta lasted for several days after Easter, and often in the evening musicians played in the plaza. Juanito's father brought his guitar and joined four or five friends who had brought their instruments, too: violins, guitars, and a cello. In the starry night you could hear them up to the very tops of the hills that surrounded the town.

Juanito sat with his mother in the patio tonight.

"It's been a long time since we had such music in the plaza," the woman said. "When your father was young he was always playing his guitar like that. He used to come and serenade me beneath my window."

"I hope Kenny and Tito hear the music," Juanito answered.

"Of course they do, if they are not too busy packing up. Tomorrow they go away."

"Don't you think it would be nice if the musicians serenaded them tonight then," Juanito asked, "if papá and the others went to play beneath their windows?"

"It's just the thing, Juanito," she said. "Let's go ask papá."

"All right. I want to see Tito's picture, too, if we go to the house."

"Of course we will. We must tell Mr. and Mrs. Strange good-bye."

She drew her shawl tighter around her shoulders and wrapped one end about her neck and head as they went through the patio, opened the gate, and hurried down the steep street.

They walked very quietly through the dusk, but they lost no time. Their bare feet slapped the cobblestones briskly with every stride.

Soon they were passing the booths and shops of the plaza. Food was still frying on the charcoal stoves. The displays of candy were not all gone, and there were even a few fragrant flowers left in the baskets. The vendors were offering them very cheaply, now that evening had come.

"We'll carry some flowers," Señora Carmen said.

"That will be fine," Juanito murmured.

They crossed the plaza toward the cathedral. A circle of people had surrounded the musicians, crowding as close as they could get to them. Juanito and his mother waited for their song to end. Then they pushed up to Señor Pérez and whispered in his ear.

"Listen, papá. Mr. and Mrs. Strange and Kenny are packing up tonight to leave Taxco. Couldn't you have the musicians come serenade them after they have finished playing here?"

"I'll ask the men," he whispered. "I'm sure they'd be glad to do it."

76

He went to each of the players, speaking softly. Then when he had spoken to all, including the cellist who stood at the far end of the group, he returned to his wife and Juanito.

"They say they'll be happy to do it," he said. "Will you both come?"

"We'll go along ahead if you don't mind. We want to see the painting of Tito Mrs. Strange has made. And we are going to carry her some flowers."

Señor Pérez thought that was a fine idea, so he slipped some pennies into Juanito's hand and a few brighter coins into the hand of his wife. By that time the musicians were ready to play another song. Juanito and his mother left the group and walked around the plaza looking for flowers that pleased them.

The night was warm and starry and full of music. And the little flares that lighted the street stands sometimes looked like twinkling stars that had fallen down to earth.

Juanito filled his arms with carnations and his mother bought a basket of yellow roses at the corner of the plaza. A few minutes later they knocked at the door of Kenny's house and Concha let them in.

Everything was topsy-turvy. Suitcases were lying open in the middle of the floor. There were two enormous bags that had been packed but not locked. There was a box of painting materials and a stack of pictures ready to be packed.

Juanito and Kenny sat together on a box kicking their feet against the sides. The older people told each other how much they hated to part, and the Stranges kept saying they liked Taxco and did not

77

wish to leave. Mrs. Strange put her face in the basket of roses, trying to take in all their sweetness at once. Her husband pinned a carnation in his wife's hair and one in the glossy black coils of the Mexican women, Concha and Señora Pérez.

After a while Juanito's mother said, "We were anxious to see your picture of Tito."

"Oh, I must show it to you," Mrs. Strange cried. "Dear, brave little Tito."

She looked through her canvases quickly and brought out a frame about four feet high. She placed it on a chair in the far corner of the room and turned the light so that it would show the picture as well as possible. There painted in oils as big as a real man stood the pasteboard bandit! His rabbit whiskers bristled magnificently. His little fist was raised as if to strike. His huge sombrero sat proudly on the back of his head. His startled eyes were as round as saucers. Everybody looked at it with admiration, saying nothing. It was a fine picture of Tito, bright and beautiful, and very jolly.

In the corner of the room, however, standing beside the red geranium in his flower pot, Tito thought of himself and imagined things that none of the others could possibly imagine. Sometimes, when he was very, very happy, he was inclined to think that he'd rather be a tiny pasteboard bandit than a real man. And that is what he was thinking tonight, having had his portrait painted, and such a fuss made over him.

"It's a wonderful picture," Juanito said.

"We have fallen in love with Tito," Mr. Strange said. "We can scarcely bear the thought of leaving him when we go."

"He is yours," Juanito said quickly. "I want Kenny to have him. Maybe—how do you say it?"

"Oh, I know what you mean," Mrs. Strange said. "You mean he'll make us think of you. Isn't that it?"

Juanito was too shy to say any more. He bowed his head.

"Thank you," Kenny said in Spanish, "*Muchas gracias*, Juanito."

Just then there was a burst of music in the street outside. Everyone paused a moment. Then the American family realized that they were being serenaded, and they all ran to the windows and out onto the balcony to listen.

There in the steep cobblestoned little street stood five or six Mexicans, their serapes thrown over their shoulders, their clothes very white in the soft darkness. Their heads were back and the sweetest of music came from their instruments as their voices were lifted in song, an old, old Mexican song.

When the singing ceased, Myrna Strange exclaimed, "How beautiful!" Then she threw them a rose, a rose for each man.

They played and sang several more songs there in the street.

Then the Americans invited the men in and offered them refreshments. For the third time everybody began to say how sad it was to part, and how much Taxco would miss them, as Juanito and Kenny sat on a box drinking fruit juice from large earthen mugs and kicking their feet against the sides. Tito stood beside them, looking across the room at his picture.

The next morning Kenny and his mother and father caught the bus in front of the cathedral. Their bags were piled on top, and they went away, waving good-bye from the windows.

"*Adiós!*" Juanito shouted as the bus departed. "*Adiós*, Kenny! *Adiós!*"

CHAPTER 12

WASHINGTON SQUARE

The bus carried the Strange family to Mexico City. There they caught a train. Throughout the journey Tito stood at the car window and looked out. He had never traveled before and everything he saw was new and wonderful. In one field there was a loaded ox cart, in another a group of children chasing butterflies. On a country road a man was carrying a bag of charcoal bigger than himself, and in a tiny crumbling village a little girl was sliding down a stone banister as the train whizzed by.

Tito noticed that the country was mostly mountainous, with dizzy slopes, deep

valleys and high peaks. He noticed that the train skirted many towns rather than going through them, and this deprived him of some of the sights. Yet he did see a few villages close up. He got a good look at the narrow streets, the high adobe walls, and the flower pots in tall grilled windows. It was a great experience for little Tito, who had never known any town but Taxco.

Whenever the train passed a village station, he saw country people lined up along the tracks. Some were sitting on horses. Some waved their big sombreros. All of them seemed happy watching the train. But what little Tito thought was that they had all come down to the tracks just to see him!

Poor little Tito, he had been praised so much since he saved the boys from the mine! He had been so flattered by having his picture painted as big as a real man that he thought all this waving of hats and serapes was just for him. He clinched his fist as tight as he could. Was he making a good impression? Of course he was!

At mealtime the train usually stopped and the passengers got out to stroll along the platform and buy tamales, enchiladas, or tacos. Some of the travelers sat down on little stools and ordered dinners at the out-of-doors tables beside the tracks when they had time.

There was much to see and Tito's bright little eyes missed nothing on the road till finally one afternoon, while Kenny was asleep, Mrs. Strange decided that the small pasteboard man had been at the window quite long enough. He was getting all dusty so she took him and tucked him away in a suitcase. That ended his fun, and the rest of the journey was hot and tiresome.

When the train crossed the border at Laredo and entered the United States, a customs officer opened the suitcase, and Tito thought for a moment that he was going to get out. But the man only unwrapped the paper enough to take one peep at the little bandit. Then he put him back in his place and locked the suitcase.

Tito didn't know how many days passed. But when he saw daylight again, he was in New York. Kenny and his mother and father were in their big studio on Washington Square with a circle of friends. Many strangers took Tito in their hands and admired his bushy whiskers and his bright clothes, as they talked about Mexico.

The next day Kenny carried the little fellow to the front window and stood him where he could look down on the Square. Later Tito heard the boy's feet on the stairs. He wondered where Kenny was going. In the street below there were many cars and taxicabs and trucks. On the sidewalks there were many people passing. In the Square there were pigeons near the fountain and children on the walks and old people on the benches. It was almost like a Mexican plaza, except busier, and there were no palm trees.

Suddenly Tito saw a familiar boy on a scooter. The boy stopped at the fountain and looked up at the window where Tito stood. He waved his hand. Yes, it was Kenny! Tito felt perfectly happy.

He knew that he would never get tired of looking out of that window with so many people below, with so many things to watch. But he couldn't help wishing that Juanito, too, had been there among the youngsters in the Square. It was really too bad that Taxco was so far from New York, he thought. And in another country, that you had to cross mountains and rivers to reach.

But one day Tito heard Blyth and Myrna Strange tell Kenny that they were going to publish a book about Mexico and put the big painting of him, Tito, in it in full colors.

"And I'll send the book to Juanito," Kenny said, "for a present."

As Tito heard this he could have laughed for joy, except that a little pasteboard bandit cannot laugh—that is, not out loud. So he just remained quiet and smiled to himself.

Once Kenny thought he caught him smiling, but then he noticed that the window was open a little and the wind just seemed to be tickling his mustache.

"Good old Tito!" Kenny said, picking him up. "Maybe next year we'll go back to Mexico again—all the way to Taxco to see our friend Juanito. How would you like that, heh?"

"Fine," Tito said—to himself.

85

AFTERWORD

CHERYL A. WALL

An inveterate traveler, Langston Hughes found himself in sympathy with the struggles of poor people wherever he went. His ports of call included Dakar, Havana, Naples, Paris, and Vladivostok. Arna Bontemps, a descendant of Louisiana Creoles who grew up in Los Angeles, was also conversant with many cultures, although his family responsibilities kept him mostly in the United States. Bontemps traveled the world through books and through conversation and correspondence with his friend Hughes. Both were proud "race men"; that is, in their lives and art they were dedicated to the advancement and freedom of black Americans. But their vision was not provincial. They were acutely aware of the common cause African Americans shared with people of color around the globe. Although *The Pasteboard Bandit* is, as Hughes called it, "a fantasy with lots of humor," it reflects its authors' social and political commitments.

On July 3, 1935, Langston Hughes wrote to an editor in the children's department of Macmillan Publishing Company, describing the manuscript he had sent her the day before. *The Pasteboard Bandit* was a children's story with a Mexican setting. Hughes expressed the hope that "our little book has some of the flavor of the country in it." Not surprisingly, it did, for he possessed a deep, firsthand knowledge of Mexico and an abiding love for its life and culture.

Hughes had first visited Mexico at the age of five, when his estranged parents attempted a reconciliation there. His father, an attorney fluent in

Spanish, amassed a small fortune in Mexico; he owned houses in Toluca and Mexico City and a ranch in Temexcaltepic. James Hughes hated American racism *and* black Americans; Mexico provided sanctuary from both. The family reunion proved short-lived. Langston did not return to his father until the summer of 1919, when he was 17 years old. According to Hughes's biographer Arnold Rampersad, it was not a happy time. The son hated the philistine in the father; the father hated the poet in the son. Nevertheless, Langston returned again to Toluca the following summer. Making his way south by train, he wrote one of his classic poems, "The Negro Speaks of Rivers."

In Toluca, he began an intensive study of Spanish; Hughes would later translate into English poems by Nicolás Guillén, Gabriela Mistral, and Federico García Lorca, among other writers. He recoiled from the plan his father mapped out for his life: engineering school in Switzerland or Germany followed by permanent expatriation in Mexico. As his father wished, Langston spent the next year in Toluca, but, defiantly, he devoted himself to writing poems that celebrated African-American identity, including "Aunt Sue's Stories," and "Mother to Son." He also began submitting his work to *The Brownies' Book*, a magazine for African-American children founded by W. E. B. Du Bois. Du Bois oversaw this venture, as he did *The Crisis*, the official publication of the National Association for the Advancement of Colored People (NAACP), with the assistance of Jessie Redmon Fauset, herself a poet and fiction writer. Fauset wrote Hughes, asking him if he had any original Mexican stories for children or perhaps could write about Mexican games. Hughes, whose strained relations with his father never affected his love for the people and lore of Mexico, complied. "Mexican Games" and "In a Mexican City," an account of life in Toluca, were published in *The Brownies' Book* in 1921.

Hughes returned to Mexico a third time in December 1934, to settle his father's affairs; James Hughes had died on October 22, 1934. Disinherited according to his father's will, Langston did benefit from this trip by drawing, once again, on the rich heritage of Mexico. He socialized with many writers and artists and was inspired by their application of modernist techniques to indigenous cultural traditions. He also shared their allegiance to leftist politics. As always, the poet of the blues responded intensely to the masses, and it is their influence that informs *The Pasteboard Bandit*. When Hughes departed from Mexico City for Los Angeles in the late spring, he packed the first draft of the manuscript.

Hughes was off to see his longtime friend and confidant, Bontemps. They had jointly written *Popo and Fifina*, a children's story set in Haiti; published in 1932, it continued to sell well. Bontemps, who had grown up with Mexican-American neighbors, and who had taught high-school Spanish, was an ideal collaborator for this book as well.

After three years of teaching at a Seventh-Day Adventist school, Oakwood Junior College, in Huntsville, Alabama, Bontemps had recently moved back to Los Angeles with his wife, Alberta, and their three children. They shared cramped quarters with Bontemps's father and stepmother. The elder Bontemps, a minister in the Seventh-Day Adventist church, sternly disapproved of his son's literary pursuits. Yet Arna Bontemps, like Hughes, was steadfast in his determination to be a writer. The problem was that on the one hand, Bontemps could not make a living from his words; on the other, those same words kept him in hot water not only with his father but with the school administrators who paid his wages. At two different schools—in Harlem and in Alabama—he had been ordered to burn the books in his home library. He refused and moved on. Without a steady income for the academic year 1934–35, he had worked on the novel, *Black Thunder*, that would win him the greatest critical praise of his career when it was published in 1936. But, for the moment, he was at loose ends.

Both born in 1902 and resembling each other enough that they were frequently mistaken for each other, Bontemps and Hughes had met in New York in 1924, during the heady days of the Harlem Renaissance. Earlier that year Bontemps had resigned his job in the Los Angeles post office and headed for Harlem, soon after his first published poem, "Hope," was accepted by *The Crisis*. Bontemps's poems were often meditative. Many, like "Golgotha is a Mountain" and "Nocturne at Bethesda," employed biblical imagery. The two poets quickly became fast friends. As Bontemps wrote in "The Awakening: A Memoir," published as the introduction to his anthology *The Harlem Renaissance Remembered* (New York: Dodd, Mead, 1972), Hughes "initiated early in 1925 a correspondence that continued uninterrupted until the week he went to the hospital for the last time in 1967." Their letters, collected in the volume *Arna Bontemps–Langston Hughes Letters* (New York: Dodd, Mead, 1980), edited by Charles Nichols, offer an incomparable account of black literary history.

By the early 1930s, Bontemps had turned his hand to prose. His first novel, *God Sends Sunday* (1931), depicted the world of the black sporting class. To Bontemps's fundamentalist employers, the title sounded blasphemous and the racetrack setting reeked of sin. Worse for Bontemps, the book suffered mixed reviews and poor sales. Determined still to be a professional writer, he turned to the field of children's literature. He sought the advice of teachers and librarians. In 1934, his first solo effort, *You Can't Pet a Possum*, earned good reviews. Buoyed by that success, Bontemps hoped to develop a series of books based on the adventures of his favorite Uncle Buddy, who had introduced him to African-American folklore. At the same time, he looked forward to collaborating again with Hughes.

In June 1935, Bontemps and Hughes rushed to complete *The Pasteboard Bandit.* After 10 days at their respective typewriters, squeezed into the already crowded Bontemps home, they were done. Hughes wrote his editor at Macmillan that librarians in Los Angeles "report an active interest in, and a shortage of books about Mexico for children." Their desperate finances along with the importuning of the publisher's West Coast representative had misled the authors into believing that the book might be accepted in time for fall publication. In a final flourish, Hughes promised another editor that "the Pasteboard Bandit himself and two of his paper-maché friends are coming on to you by express from Los Angeles." He hoped that the toys he had purchased in Mexico the previous winter might inspire an illustrator. He had someone in mind: Miguel Covarrubias, the Mexican-born artist who had illustrated Hughes's first book, *The Weary Blues,* in 1926 and who, Hughes vouched, had "both color and a grand sense of humor."

Three weeks later, *Pasteboard's* hopes were dashed. A rejection letter came from Macmillan stating that despite the "interesting background material," the story was not strong enough to hold the attention of younger readers. The manuscript had been read and rejected, while the editor with whom Hughes and Bontemps had worked previously was on vacation. When she returned, she enclosed a copy of the confidential readers' reports with her note. Neither evaluator liked the manuscript. One found fault with the shifting point of view; the other expected something different from two poets who were "members of a feeling race."

Hughes and Bontemps did not miss a beat. That same month they submitted a second children's book manuscript, "Bon-Bon Buddy," which was summarily rejected. In years to come, their luck would change. Among their joint efforts are the landmark anthologies, *The Poetry of the Negro, 1746–1949* and *The Book of American Negro Folklore.* Individually, they continued to write for children. Hughes published *Famous Negro Heroes*, *The First Book of Jazz*, and *The First Book of Rhythms*, among many others. Bontemps's titles include *Golden Slippers: An Anthology of Negro Poetry for Young Readers*, *The Story of the Negro*, and *Free at Last: The Life of Frederick Douglass*; this last book was published in 1971, two years before Bontemps's death. In an undated letter, probably written in the late 1930s, Bontemps wrote Hughes that the author of a textbook on children's literature had contacted him. She wanted permission to excerpt a section of *Popo and Fifina*. It seemed, Bontemps continued, that the two old friends were "going to be models for future generations of writers for children and students of that literature." They have turned out to be just that.

The Pasteboard Bandit is a story of cultural interaction and exchange. It balances the representation of Mexican and U.S. cultures by telling its story largely from the toy bandit's point of view. While the disapproving editors of yesteryear might have yearned for a staunch Yankee perspective, the Hughes-Bontemps creation, Tito, mediates between the Mexican and American characters. For example, he understands both Spanish and English, and "it made no difference at all to him" which one was spoken. The casual incorporation of Spanish words into the story reinforces the point that each language is acceptable. At the end of the book, when the Mexican child, Juanito, makes a present of the bandit to his American friend, Kenny, Tito travels to New York. Washington Square becomes as much a site of difference as the Mexican village of Taxco.

That the New Yorkers are surnamed "Strange" underscores the novel's theme of cultural relativism. To Juanito, the Americans are peculiar. *His* experiences are the norm. By introducing the Pérez family first, the novel lessens the tendency for the U.S. reader to identify with the Strange family. The novel does not value one culture above the other. For example, the story ascribes equal worth to Señor Pérez's vernacular art (his painted gourds and pottery) and the paintings of the American couple. In one of several scenes depicting Christmas in Mexico, the hosts invite the Stranges to join in the festivities. Reversing the usual expectations, the Mexicans judge the folk poems and songs ("Oh, Susannah" and "Listen to the Mocking Bird") that the Americans perform for them. By the end of his sojourn in Taxco, the young American concludes that "a piñata's almost as good as a Christmas tree, except that it hasn't got candles." He has learned the bandit's lessons well.

Tito exemplifies the values of tolerance, courage, and pride that the story endorses. Momentarily disappointed by the poverty of the Pérez family when he is brought into their home, he immediately reminds himself that it "did not matter if they were very kind and polite." The parents prove exemplary in every way; the story depicts their deep concern for their son by providing details of the mother's loving preparation of food and the father's careful restoration of the bandit. Tito has earned this attention by the act of bravery that saves the boys. Even when his colors fade and the papier-mâché begins to crumble, his dignity remains intact.

At the book's conclusion, Kenny's parents are planning to publish a book about Mexico that will contain a full-color portrait of "the Pasteboard Bandit." This was, of course, the authors' plan. In 1942 Hughes donated the manuscript of *The Pasteboard Bandit* to the James Weldon Johnson Collection at Yale University. Above the date and his signature, he wrote the words "as yet unpublished." Now, at long last, *The Pasteboard Bandit* has arrived.

Langston Hughes (1902–1967) was born in Joplin, Missouri, and grew up in Kansas, Illinois, and Ohio. He traveled to Mexico several times to visit his estranged father and was greatly affected by the people and lore of Mexico. He later traveled all over the world—to Europe, Africa, the Soviet Union—but his heart and home were in Harlem, where he was one of the most versatile writers of the artistic movement known as the Harlem Renaissance. Though known primarily as a poet, Hughes also wrote plays, essays, novels, short stories, and books for children, including *The First Book of Rhythms, Famous Negro Heroes of America,* and *Black Misery.*

Arna Bontemps (1902–1973) was born in Louisiana and grew up in California. He moved to New York City in 1923, and it was there that he met Langston Hughes and other writers who were leaders of the Harlem Renaissance. Bontemps began his literary career as a poet but also wrote novels, edited anthologies of African-American poetry and folktales, and wrote many popular children's books, including *Slappy Hooper, The Fast Sooner Hound,* and *Popo and Fifina* (coauthored with Hughes). While known as one of our major African-American poets, Bontemps is also credited with making black folklore and literature available to the public through his anthologies and through his work as a historian, librarian, and teacher at several American universities.

Peggy Turley is also the illustrator of the acclaimed picture book *Armadillo Ray*. She holds a B.A. in history from the University of Memphis, where she also studied painting and photography. She lives in Memphis with her daughters, Ginny and Betsy.

Alex Bontemps, one of Arna Bontemps's six children, teaches history at Dartmouth College. His research centers on African Americans in the colonial period.

Cheryl A. Wall is professor of English at Rutgers University. She is the author of *Women of the Harlem Renaissance* and the editor of *Zora Neale Hurston: Novels and Stories*.

Robert G. O'Meally is Zora Neale Hurston Professor of American Literature at Columbia University and previously taught English and Afro-American studies at Wesleyan University and Barnard College. He is the author of *The Craft of Ralph Ellison* and *Lady Day: Many Faces of the Lady* and editor of *Tales of the Congaree by E. C. Adams* and *New Essays on "Invisible Man."* Professor O'Meally is coeditor of *History and Memory in African-American Culture* and *Critical Essays on Sterling A. Brown.*

THE IONA AND PETER OPIE LIBRARY
OF CHILDREN'S LITERATURE

The Opie Library brings to a new generation an exceptional selection of children's literature, ranging from facsimiles and new editions of classic works to lost or forgotten treasures— some never before published—by eminent authors and illustrators. The series honors Iona and Peter Opie, the distinguished scholars and collectors of children's literature, continuing their lifelong mission to seek out and preserve the very best books for children.

ROBERT G. O'MEALLY, GENERAL EDITOR